# THE IMAGINED REALITY

## "PURSUING YOUR REAL WISDOM IN ROUTINE AISLE"

SHUBHANGI SAXENA

THE IMAGINED REALITY

"PURSUING YOUR REAL WISDOM IN ROUTINE AISLE"

by

SHUBHANGI

SAXENA

PART 1

## ABOUT THE AUTHOR

SHUBHANGI SAXENA

*Academician, Certified Life Coach & Leadership Development Consultant*

As an Achology Certified Life Coach with a Postgraduation in Hospitality & Tourism Management, Shubhangi partner with leaders to develop their executive presence, and strategic communication skills in order to reach individual and organizational goals.

Shubhangi Saxena's Forte in Interview Preparation, Leadership Development, Business Communication, Management Training as well as English Fluency makes her Passionate and Effective Mentor for Grooming Future Leaders and Students from varied set of Disciplines and walks, students and Clients have consistently recommended Shubhangi, citing her as a trusted and empowering coach, strategic and creative thinker, and direct and compassionate communicator. Shubhangi has a warm, motivating way of challenging students and holding them accountable for designing and sustaining meaningful change.

I provide customized solutions for leaders and organizations. This approach includes assessments, feedback, and inquiry to generate insights and a development plan based on strengths, needs, and gaps. While the specifics of the approach look different for each leader, my clients and I always focus on integrating their states of "being" and "doing." When these two align, profound leaps in leadership become possible.

As Albert Einstein said, "The mind that opens to a new idea never returns to its original size." We couldn't agree more. Shubhangi has always been fascinated by human behaviour, cultures, and the way people live and work around the world. Traveling to varied locations has broadened her perspective; this expansive way of thinking influences her coaching style, she blends her Leadership experience with her Education in Hospitality & Tourism and extensive background in mindfulness, to support clients' growth through challenges and change. Shubhangi herself has Aced several Top-Notch campus Placements during her Management Recruitment Drive and possess strong interpersonal skills.

Shubhangi is a Faculty, Life Coach & A Hospitality Enthusiast and enjoy leading workshops, trainings, keynotes, and retreats about

Leadership.

Specialties & Strengths: Executive coaching, Leadership development, Leadership training & facilitation, Team building, experiential learning, Leadership coaching, Business communication

## CONTENTS OF THE REALITY

1. LET'S BEGIN (One who resists can only do it)

1. TRUE WISHES (It all begins with it)

3. OVERCOMING FEAR OF FAILURE (It stays with everyone so learn to deal with it)

## #1

## LET'S BEGIN

### "ONE WHO RESISTS CAN ONLY DO IT"

Our imagination is everything, Great things are always difficult to imagine initially but when these imagined things are clubbed with meaning, patience and perseverance, they could create miracle and all the material things that we ever imagined.

A couple of years ago, someone in the northwest of France in the name of Bella Charles discovered the imagined thoughts of reality and wisdom. The thought wasn't just a nocturnal discovery but the outcome of years of hard work and persistence of Bella in trying to discover the real light of success and imagination. Everything started with her wide meeting with Anna Carver, A successful but soft-hearted Entrepreneur and business lady of her own fad.

The most wonderful quality of Bella was her uncertain fear of change. She discovered Anna and her great life story and carefully crafted a well-furnished plan on how to achieve all the imagined stuff she aspired throughout her life and to well understand this one has to understand the further steps to imagined reality on how to become more successful and famous.

This was the time when Bella was imagining her realities of being the most successful, the very first time this thought ran in her mind she resisted to act upon. She surrounded herself with certain irreversible doubts. Out of all her doubts three major ones were – How to reach Anna, and if she reaches her how to please Anna and last but not the least how to impress her in the first ongoing conversation.

These three ongoing doubts were enough to let that resistance stop her from reaching the imagined reality as these thoughts can astray any women from taking first step in faith. But Bella was someone with no extraordinary resistance that paves towards great outcomes. And that is when she decided to contact her friend Isabella who was girlfriend to a man named Bennett – Personal Assistant to Ms. Anna Carver. To her surprise Bella finally got her chance, the very first chance to meet Ms. Anna Carver.

The day at Anna's office Entrance, Bella dressed herself in the best of the clothing she could, so that she could make her way to Ms. Anna mind as a future Entrepreneur, Anna entered the office entrance in her flawless attire as she always looks, just wow. Anna was standing near entrance like a "moron of speechless thought" as she just browsed Anna only in Business magazines or Interviews. Anna could see there is some ordinary girl looks like waiting for her to speak to with her glazed eyes of a long wait. Bella was just an ordinary tramp but Anna could see the sparkle of something different in her eyes like she came here to accomplish the imagined reality.

After a considerable and generous moment of weird silence. Anna asked her who she is and what brought her here to Anna's office. Now what Bella answered to Anna at that moment was completely generous to what Anna could have ever said to herself or imagined. And trust Anna it wasn't Bella's innocent face that Anna couldn't refuse but the depth of the thoughtful sentences that Bella restored in Anna's head.

At that time Bella didn't get through the deal of working with Anna, as it was her very first effort of getting towards. Bella couldn't even made Anna that impressed of being able to work in her office as a receptionist or petty wage worker, reason being Bella mentioned about her concept of reaching towards imagined reality by extreme hard work and justice while utilising her very first chance of conversation that she could make at the Entrance.

Anna wanted to hear of Bella that how she could manipulate her thoughts into vision of imagined success and wisdom and while doing that what would be her first step to gear ahead which Bella failed to explain to her and the opportunity was dismissed as "opportunities are one time and one moment game "of either achieving everything or being nowhere in the world of false paradise as they say.

Weeks after weeks Bella kept thinking what went wrong that she was completely unheard. Seemingly Bella couldn't discover the reason and nothing great happened while all the time went off. At the same time only one amazing desire was burning that was in the heart of Bella to get into the office of Anna Carver as she wanted to make it possible anyhow and by any means, with weeks and time passing by the desire was getting more intense and justified as it seems to Bella.

And then as this chapter says and I believe that "One who resists can only do it" and that burning desire of getting there stays with these reluctant people only. Bella was completely ready for a new revolution of reaching the imagined reality and so she was all set to get along with Anna as her personal manager until Bella gets the way out of reaching her goal of pursuing success, something Bella was seeking in and out and everywhere.

After working for a while with Anna Carver, Bella could have had easily been telling herself that" she's just doing this personal manager job for lame reason" and I'll get experience from here and will try for something better at some different organization but she only kept telling herself every now and then that, she arrived here for a definite purpose of becoming a business lady like that of Ms. Anna carver and will learn each and everything from Anna until she achieves her goal, no matter whatever it takes. "Bella was specific and meant it" If you decide on a Goal and get a lot of struggles on the way while making it then don't be disappointed instead keep reminding yourself the reason why you are here, as one who remembers the root never fails to achieve the best!

And as they say" When you attract something with true determination and desire it ultimately comes to you sooner or later", Bella barely had any idea about the opportunity moving towards her direction of determination and persistence. But then there is a beautiful habit of all the great opportunities as when they come to you they always appear like a bloom doom and they trick you towards something odd which gets you sly down and makes you feel worthless may be the meaning of opportunities is basically a bit roller coaster ride, initially they won't let you enjoy the ride but once you have learned to control and balance the wheels the ride is ever joyful. Actually, this is the Probable reason why all of us fail to recognize the opportunity.

The opportunity was subtle "Ms Anna decided to launch a new product in her genre of Beauty" Initially no one from her company had good gut feeling about this Product and nobody truly had a belief in Anna's new product and launching it to the market was quite a trouble that all her employees projected. The sales projection of the new product was in doom already but all of this was happening in presence of Bella and she could clearly see an opportunity to be in the shoes of Anna and proving her product as the best.

Bella was confident enough that she could sell the beauty product advertising it in the most adjective way as she learned this craft purposefully all her life being in association with Mark A.Edyln Advertising & company, The sale hour prompted on and Bella did prove her calibre, the product was an all-time hit in the market and Anna carver was so delighted by Bella's work that she gave her the entire business contract of that beauty product as it was a great miracle for Anna in all the 24 years of her Business career. Bella made an all-time great money and her dreams were all the way there approaching humbly and steadily. At that very moment she realized that dreams can be true if accompanied with Hard work and determination. All in all "The Imagined Reality" was coming true and closer.

Bella was always curious to explore things in her favour and acquire everything she ever dreamt off but when she made money as she always wanted too, the question was how much?? What was her due hunger, there was no answer for that, the good and unzippable part was amid all this chaos she discovered that "Thoughts could be things" if pursued with perseverance, passion and calibre.

Bella was on ninth cloud as she thought she is now into a business association with the only Ms. Anna Carver! She didn't have had any idea of the journey ahead but she did know that this is the track to walk ahead, she was a terrific believer in destiny and fortune was all her way kissing hands. Her firm believe was getting her all that she wanted and finally she sailed great on the journey in front and forth.

There are possible angles of the same situation, being a life coach, I've known people who would believe in every sign of them getting closer towards their goals but then when they embark on the journey of materializing these "thought into things" the obvious obstacles haunt them and all the signs of their success are lost somewhere in false darkness of never coming true. And they give up badly one even the very initial idea of chasing their goals.

Buying it for ten thousand Euros

Imagination is the biggest motivator towards achieving real life success, simply because our brain cannot make a difference if thoughts are just thoughts or the ultimate reality" Thoughts are things" And some way or the other Imagined reality always stays on and on.

While being on the trip to life for 26 years, and meeting hundreds of people as Professional and as freelancer, I realised that the most certain reasons of failure and agony in every step towards career & life is the habit of leaving the room just by opening it's door, the context is most of us "The witty" us decide to give up on our goals just by facing a random façade of initial failure and trust me each one of us have been through this toxic pattern and only tough barrier towards a healthy career and relationships.

Rose has always been enticed by gems and luxury, maybe that's why she attended the IFA fashion school at Paris to achieve her degree in fashion and Jewellery designing, she really knew well to adore the most precious and beautiful gems into her artwork. Rose was always committed towards achieving big and opening her own diamond jewellery store at saint Peterson aisle and to her surprise she got an offer from a famous Jewellery brand "The Crystal" as they wanted rose's services for their artwork designing.

After working with "The Crystal" for more than six months, Rose designed a masterpiece of Gemstone Jewellery and presented it to Mr. Mike (The Crystal CEO) in private affair as she was planning something parallelly while designing the masterpiece, Mike was always been supportive and trusted the calibre of Rose.

Rose was always certain that her Artwork is a hidden masterpiece and it will yield a lot of profit and fortune to Rose as she had a good pile of debt over her head and regular bills to pay off, and then would arrive the big killings in profits, But to her surprise when she arrived in the Jewellery fare everything seem so down as she could gaze the most scrumptious masterpieces are all aligned to showcase and her hope was carving down the aisle, Then Mike appeared and his charismatic words cheered up Rose to the level up of the hopes, she stood in the showcase and displayed her masterpiece work "The Gemstone Jewellery" and the buyers were gathered to see that masterpiece, its ultimate crafting, the beauty it holds and much more, the work was altogether appreciated and people started asking for the price, Rose dictated Eighty thousand Euros and it barely took few seconds as she could gaze at the changed expressions of people pulling strings of appreciation so far went in ultimate sense of oblivious pattern.

Within no time rose realized that people were allured to her masterpiece artwork because they were assuming it to be very low priced, Mike and Rose tried harder to explain the worth of the masterpiece but all in vain, they both decided to stay up for the hours till the fare could end and may be some catch could be arrived up by here and there but soon the fare hours were over and they both had to come to the end of the rainbow as the worthy customers and adorning morons were no longer there and Rose was still hoping to get that right catch---- All out in vain.

Finally, they were on the one and only pick to quit.

They sold the masterpiece to the last buyer named "Nicolas" of the showcase for ten thousand dollars the last price they could think of getting for her all-time hard work & Precious craft, Mike dropped rose home and left for his own setup at "The Crystal" as he had a lot to finish before signing the day off.

The last buyer "Nicolas" did some maths going back home all night and decided to take the Masterpiece Jewellery to his friend and Jewellery store owner "Charles" who was keenly interested in curating masterpieces of jewellery and specially Gemstone was his all-time found. Nicolas presented the Masterpiece to Charles asking him to find out the real price, after considerable time towards gazing the Masterpiece for minutes Charles spoke up Hey man! It's worth A lakh Euros, Nicolas could barely believe his ears and asked Charles to repeat what he just said and Charles again in ecstatic symphony yelled, It's worth one lakh dollars! That's exactly what Charles recited.

Nicolas sold the jewellery to Charles franchise store and made one lakh Euros out of Ten thousand Euros bargained ones which he bought from Rose last night" The hopeless lady of masterpiece". The last buyer could make all the money from that masterpiece because he knew to get into the expert advice before leaving the ride off (Giving up).

Remember why Rose and Mike couldn't get the real Price for their Hard work and lost the all-time blossoming fortune because they gave up right when it was supposed to not. The last buyer "Nicolas" had no idea about the craft and the work of masterpiece, he never went to the Jewellery designing school or had an experience of working at a jewellery store with the well-known like "The crystal" but he did know how to explore the possibilities before leaving it off for further future and Nicolas made it all time big from somebody else's work for which he had a legal ownership that night by just paying "ten thousand Euros"

Much prior to success and wisdom knocking your door, it is certain that temporary defeat and failures will be your neighbours. After coming across people from all walks of life and understanding their ultimate patterns of thick and thin, I did realise that when failure strikes the doorstep, the easiest and most ultimate step is to give up and that's what most of the wisest us do. But then the most famous and blessed money men have revealed that their greatest fortune came just a step beyond the decimal where failure was all and everywhere. Failure always weakens you and pulls you away from good fortune and success but at the same time one needs to realize that temporary and most impactful failures are just the roadblock towards a bright and shiny future, those needs to be cleared and the journey needs to be resumed!

A deep breath of coloured boy

Ms. Gladwin was a lady of worship and soon after she finished her daily prayers at" The Church of Vincent" she was keenly observing this Brat talking to tourists in the most convincing manner as he could and dictating history of the place. Ms. Gladwin was an experienced hotelier and soon after completing her hospitality education from Swiss Hotel Management school, decided to open her own hotel, she began with an embarking rock and now was running a tall building of 105 rooms and 4 banquets, she could be a better hotelier but running down towards her skill set of convincing people or getting into conversations was an "Imagined Reality" of every inch towards being a better soul.

One fine evening she planned to visit her Aunt Polly and packed her bags, on her way she was just imagining herself as the most skilful communicator while visualizing her dream of reality with closed eyes, barely did she know that this journey would communicate her inner self into the very own reality. Her Aunt operated a beauty salon over a faith of all worthy customers. All of a sudden, the salon door was opened, and a coloured boy of somewhere in the age of seventeen, the nearby coffee vendor's boy, walked inside and sat near the table folding his legs.

Aunty Polly looked towards, up gazed the boy and asked him to leave without creating much fuss as she was busy dealing with customers.

The boy meekly reverted, "You have my 100 bucks" sitting in the same position of folded legs.

Aunt Polly retorted in haste, carrying on with her work, you won't get anything, you better run on from here.

The boy said "Yes madame" but did not budge at all from there, Ms. Gladwin was just astonished seeing the ultimate confidence & courage of the teen boy at just seventeen.

While all of this run, A tourist lady from Macerata arrived at the salon and murmured something in a distinguished accent of Italy, before Aunt Polly could react over this, the teen boy smiled and replied something in the same distinguished accent and the tourist lady was seated in no time, All of us at the salon were in huge surprise trying to figure out the event just happened, the little boy whispered something in private to Aunt and she started giving Facial massage to the tourist lady, After five minutes Aunt stopped near the table gazed at the boy, put her hand in the wallet and gave two hundred bucks instead of holy hundred ones.

The teen accepted the money with valour like he has earned it with all the due respect and pushed himself back towards the exit of the door from where he entered, smiling with reminiscence breathing and gazing Aunt Polly. After he left aunty polly again picked with her work of facial massage but Ms. Gladwin was still awestruck with the trip she just had, she was doing some thinking over and again wondering if she could learn all the craft of mustering courage and dealing with people as to satisfy her imagined reality to the core of it. She never came across someone so concrete and especially being a person of colour that he mastered the white lady of age. What eclectic superpower did the teen boy possess? What did he communicate to the Tourist lady? How did he communicate being non-native speaker of Italian accent who's never been to school and barely could flaunt the language of his own? How did the dramatic and cold-hearted Aunt Polly have had a change of heart that too so sudden? Where did this teen learn all the confidence and communication thing? Many similar questions flashed into Ms. Gladwin's mind but she could not exactly figure out the answers

The very next morning, Bells rings and Aunt Polly asks Ms. Gladwin to open the door and to her surprise whom does she spot on the door, It's the same-coloured teen boy whose puzzles were still entangled in Ms. Gladwin's head. Aunt Polly yelled to ask who is it? Probably from the washroom as she was bathing at the time, Ms. Gladwin told it's the same boy who was there at the salon and the voice said, I am coming in a while.

Ms. Gladwin had the perfect opportunity to seek answers to all her questions, she offered water to the boy and asked him to sit down comfortably. The boy smiled again and looked at Ms. Gladwin like he has already read her mind through the sparkling eyes. Ms. Gladwin went on to ask, hey what do you do, the boy replied "I sell Coffee and hot dogs for a living" She further asked, do you go to school or college, The teen boy reverted meekly No I don't but I want to one fine day, this statement expelled Ms. Gladwin's curiosities to the sky high and she vividly asked then how did you learn these communication and languages, like you were talking to the Italian lady yesterday at salon" she pinpointed" Oh that, The boy chuckled a bit for this question and answered I was always keenly interested in languages and whenever tourists visited my kiosk, I used to keenly observe them talking which made me decipher things from accents like I did yesterday. He further went on to narrate his story of always imagining himself as a successful orator and Effective communicator, he told he was always interested in how people talk and live with their standards and wisdom, how they walk how, how they learn and much more

Ms. Gladwin was highly astonished to know that someone with no formal education and literacy can learn things which people try learning giving money in high repute institutions and walking through different experiences of a lifetime. The answers were complete and satisfactory when she grasped her breath for a moment wondering that everything is possible if a person is truly self-motivated and convinced for things he or she wants.

The cosmic forces can give you everything and anything all that we need is an intense desire to make a wish and all the cosmic powers will bring that to you in reality. You will catch a glimpse of this same cosmic power in the next chapter. You will also learn how to unleash your true potential by believing in these cosmic energies and frequencies, how you can make your thoughts into things in reality and achieve everything by commanding the right thing at right time.

These energies will strengthen you to begin purposefully and with all the optimism, may lead you towards success theories and might take you in the hands of failures and pessimism too, but at this time when things are happening in the opposite direction, we need to stop and think where we are and where did we come from all the while, you will understand that when it's all defeat around that's where the real results of all your hard work is going to emerge out and will bless you with everything you ever wished for as you've worked hard for it.

Within no time, Ms. Gladwin could understand the concept of convincing minds through this coloured boy which she was trying to gauge all the years of her being in hotel business and leading people from all walks of life. Soon after returning back to her Ms. Gladwin decided to be a lady of strong determination and every time that she got an opportunity to make it big with her guests, she convinced herself with the unfathomable courage she received from the teen boy and nailed it every now and then, very soon even the Guest Relation Manager who were earning in good bucks because of Ms. Gladwin's approach towards being unwitty and unwilling to convince people was also puzzled and surprised and soon was replaced by Ms. Gladwin itself as she could handle the guests herself.

Thinking back towards all those years Ms. Gladwin realised that everything that happens to you, happens for a reason and everything that she lost over the years due to her inability of convincing people and presenting herself with ideas had to be made up one day by simply coming across this coloured teen child, who without really teaching anything taught a lesson of a lifetime to Ms. Gladwin. This accomplished tale of Ms. Gladwin and the coloured boy will be read through this book by millions and billions of people especially those who are in the hunt of that one fine opportunity which would change their life and will make them emerge out as a winner in that unseen crowd but we need to understand that every opportunity and blessing will walk towards you with right time and right set of life experiences but this all comes with that undying zeal of being where you want to be.

Set your goals right and be very tight in your thoughts to accomplish it anyhow and somehow and you will see the world opening up all the arms for you and revealing the unhidden cosmic energies of success and wisdom.

Touching it to Gold

We often imagine of having special powers where we touching anything and it turns into wealth, don't' we? we all somewhere desire to make this imagination a true unforgivable reality

To explain further, let me take you towards the story of "A mighty king and his son Alexander".

After the great economic depression, the entire state was poverty stricken. Every voice was asking alexander and the king for sustainability of life, King tried everything, he asked for money from neighbouring states, even reminded his favours he did to people but all in vain, his people were dying of poverty, in the absence of basic amenities and food life was treating the kingdom in the worst of its possible scenario, the king was finding it hard to get these kingdom people survive.

Observing these ugly scenarios and finding father king helpless Alexander asked to his father, can I do something for you and the kingdom father? Within no time the dull sulking eyes of king started to glare with hope at his son Alexander, he asked in surprise, what can you do son? Alexander was already quite aware of the principles of happiness, wisdom and wealth, which will be further discussed in the coming chapters of this book.

Alexander came out to speak his sense of mind to the kingdom people and tried to make them understand the true faith of cosmic energies, he further went on and asked the kingdom people to start doing the same work of handicraft and other things that they used to do for living, he assured them that he will take all these things to other kingdoms for sale, we will all earn big and will have big feast together, All we need to do is start realizing the worth of what we have and stop worrying for what we don't have, Alexander spoke golden words and that very moment he saw a miracle happening around, the people left their worries and started to work as their humble best, Alexander had special cosmic powers of turning anything and everything that he touches into gold only if he wants too, his father even wasn't aware of these special powers alexander possessed, alexander never used these powers for the unnecessary or scrupulous intentions but here he needed to use these and he touched few assets which turned into gold, he asked his neighbouring kingdom Prince Athens for some favour of arranging material things and food for his kingdom people in exchange of these gold assets and within no time, the things were arranged, people started working and the handicrafts were super ready.

At the same time alexander's great connections in talking to merchants or buyers of the handicrafts to visit his kingdom displayed results, soon one merchant from foreign land bought all the material craft for 50 times more money than the kingdom people and alexander ever imagined, the gradual spell of darkness soon changed into the light of happiness before they realized it, and the uncertain fear of people's mind was transmuted into intense faith and harmony.

What we need to understand here is, as early as we begin diving into these principles of impracticality or irreversible cosmic energies, we will start achieving wealth and happiness in abundance and everything that we touch will become an important asset for our happiness and benefit.

But most of the time we refuse to believe in these very theories, in fact there is a very obvious belief that we are all been nurtured with, which depicts that wealth and wisdom is the only accomplishment of hard work or simply working in sweat and blood. But as we go through this journey of imaginations and truly accomplishing thoughts into material things, we need to have faith in our minds not in our hard work, yes, the true imagination can turn anything into reality once our mind starts to possess wealth through thoughts as the study of years revealed that our brain cannot really differ between imagination and reality, as if we are just thinking of doing it or we are actually doing it.

I was always interested in knowing how people become wealthy, what's that hidden talent that they have to succeed on grounds of wealth and wisdom. After considerable research of more than 10 years into this practice I came across some very true impressions that these people possess, we can all be very wealthy not just in terms of wealth but on every aspect of our fortunate chapters of a journey called Life.

Moving ahead I came realising that the most significant reasons of human suffering is the feeling of doubtfulness and the lack of faith, we humans possibly know every rule which will not work in our favour and are truly inclined towards the better word of their innate dictionary "Not possible" This book is an amalgamation of all those rules and stories which will derive you to abundance and success.

Success is a result not an effort, especially in today's world when competition is a definition to success, we need to read this book and realise where are we exactly heading and where do we need to merge our directions because wealth and happiness comes to those who really strive for it and truly want it.

And failure is nothing but a gift of our own pessimistic thoughts, we become apprehensive about our own hopeful efforts exactly when they are about to grow into larger results of wisdom and within no time the success is turned into failure.

This book will guide you towards the basic elements of not entering the danger zone of pessimism and where to enter right towards the safest zone called the zone of wisdom, learning on being more confident and faithful towards achieving the goals. combined research on humans prove that they are accustomed to gauge everything they pursue towards achievement of goals and this calculated theory without involvement of risks is dangerous habit for achieving big and better.

I know thousands of minds who are reading this book might feel miserable as they think themselves deeply rooted in pessimistic thoughts by their routine actions such as fighting with someone every day, being rude and cheeky at workplace, bargaining and abusing at grocery store, finding flaws in good things, never appreciating people for their kindness, making your spouse feel degraded or substandard, never smiling back, asking for unnecessary favours, always being apprehensive, being disloyal and dishonest, being greedy, commanding everyone around and much more.

Having a replica like Queensland Palace

There were a couple of architects & engineers who were asked to built a Mansion just as the replica of Queensland Palace where prince Matthew lived for 90 years, Initially these people declined the request of prince Matthew's daughter Lina quoting that this replica is one and only, we cannot create it the same here as it's impossible but Lina who was just as stubborn as his father asked the masons to keep up on creating the model and do whatever it takes but she wants the same replica here in Greenwich. The blueprint was placed on paper, but the architects & engineers agreed to this lady, by saying it's absolutely impossible yet again to create the same replica.

Lina reverted, "Create it anyway" She further commanded the architects to go ahead and stay on until you are a success, take as much time as much you want but I want results on ground.

They started their work created designs & blueprints again and again, consulted facility planners and other work staff as they had nothing else to do except creating the same replica, 2 months passed but nothing was yet conceptualized. Architects & Engineers tried every way out to perform Lina's orders but all of it went in vain, after 7 months on the same verge Lina arrived to check with the architects if they have started something of have found a way to conceptualize the work on creating replica.

Liba straightaway commanded checking the work in progress, you start building the rocks and something will emerge out in the favour because anyhow you all have to follow my orders and construct the same replica of the palace, "I Have immense faith in all of you as only you can do it."

I know i will have my dream of seeing the exact palace here soon! Lina exclaimed. Having a Replica of this palace here was been imagined by Lina thousands of times and now very soon this imagination was turning out to be Lina's most awaited reality.

The architects & engineers went ahead and started construction imagining the real Palace and keeping the random piece of blueprint concept in their heads, and to all the magical fortunes, the palace replica was constructed having the same random concept and real imagination.

The story is not as short as it has been deduced here, it took good 7 years for the complete construction of the Palace, but the question is how? Especially when the architects & engineers were finding it impossible to even start constructing a stepping stone and now finally the exact replica which even looks more real than the imagination, was it Lina's immense faith in workers or the workers believed in golden words of Lina as she described faith in them. There could be many questions but answer to every question is more or less similar which says if you imagine something and truly want it in reality, everything is possible and things will work in your favour.

You can create it all with rue desire and belief in yourself, if you passionately want something, all the cosmic energies will get that thing to you, so if you want success never be disheartened by your initial failures or pessimistic routine actions, as habits could be turned into the way you want only if you truly want success and wealth, if you want to be a leader and not the path follower.

In this short story of Lina and her string determination an extremely impractical and unrealistic effort and picture has been described but if you are an opportunist, you will pick up the most adorable formulas and thoughts from this which can make you succeed in your goals and produce all the material wealth you can ever wish for.

So, believe in yourself and you will find birds chirping just for you, cuckoo singing your favourite songs and the world will turn in your favour as you always wanted it.

First copy to M

Last year in the month of June, I delivered my victory lecture at the university of Pennsylvania amid the chaos and hodge podge of a thousand appropriate audience and the topic was "stepping stones towards your ultimate goal" where I described the principles of focus and faith, on the same evening when I returned home and was browsing friends chat, A guy named M contacted me and wanted to express his part of understanding the principle taught by me in the victory lecture, he was aware that I am writing a book on the hidden principles of imagination and reality, and asked if he can meet once and share his story about the magnetic treasures this principle holds, initially I wasn't convinced but within no time I agreed to make him a part and we decided to meet at captain's café next evening 6'o.

The next evening, I was right on time but he seems to have been joining in a while, within little time while I was pondering my eyes all around in the café, A six feet man with a graceful white skin and shiny big eyes, little calming demeanour walked towards me and introduced himself as M, we Shaked hands and went on to share each other's glimpse of the story we were trying to interpret.

The young man was heading his own successful business of cartridges and other explosives, he explained his understanding of the principle with so much intensity and focus that I then and there decided to deliver my first copy to him as soon as the book is ready. I was imagining where was this man all the while.

He told me how he planted the big idea of turning imagination into reality and thoughts into material things and this whole idea is the result of my current opportunities and how he is serving the workers of his manufacturing units, he also stated that whatever opportunities of success he will achieve in future will be just because of these ultimate cosmic energies and the principles he learnt and has been practicing.

Listening to his piece of mind, I recalled Ms. Gladwin, Alexander and Lina's stories of strong demeanour in believing things and materializing them into reality, he told me stories of people with no professional education and wealthy backgrounds have risen to greatest of the heights and are currently wealthy not just in finances but in relationships, love and health too.

After returning home I recalled his words of wisdom several times in my head and realized that there are millions of young minds who dream and imagine of being wealthy, charismatic and successful but due to little or no knowledge about these magnetic principles they fail to transmute their big imagination theories into ground reality.

When I recite opening up my eyes in morning that " I am enough and the most fortunate person" And can create anything I want in reality, Should I familiarize these millions of people too about these charismatic principles, I should reach out to these minds to tell them how our brains can be functioned to believe what we want to ( as our brain cannot make a difference in imagination and reality) It's time when they should know how wealth can be created in abundance just by believing in yourself and the cosmic energies.

Gradually as you read this book to the end of all these chapters, you will get to see the hidden treasures of success and wealth and how everything can be chased into material things.

With no surprise, I received a call from M after seven months of writing and he asked if I can have the first copy of your book, also if you would come to deliver it from your own hands as I will be organizing the big feast for the success of this book.

I nodded in yes and now we shall move to the next chapter.

Thanks for reading this one! Have a great time practicing imagined reality.

# 2

<u>TRUE WISHES</u>

"IT ALL BEGINS WITH IT"

Dream big and don't give up

Marcia was nothing but an orphan fellow who wanted to run away from orphanage because nobody was behaved nicely to her, she was really been ill treated by the fellow orphans and other people in the facility for all the years, she was shy and fearsome, a girl who would not revert to any question asked with high pitch but would get closer to people who would behave better and would pour her heart out.

She might have had this demeanour of a loser she knew how to push her limits and reach out the path of being a Royal highness, she knew how to attract good things and people in life, humble credits to one of her maths teacher Mr. Harvard. It was one grey afternoon that she met Mr. Harvard "A man of his own presence" and to no surprise Marcia fell in love with herself as Mr. Harvard taught her this craft of imagining things in mind and seeing it around for real.

As she decided to run away from orphanage and become the person of calibre, it was no one but Mr. Harvard's magic formula that gave Marcia all the great confidence as she already imagined a picture of her life with Roman cliff (An industrialist and a descendant of royal roots).

One-night marcia packed her bags and took little cash in her pocket to take a train to Georgia, where Roman lived with her Royal surroundings, as she made her way to Georgia while crossing in numerous obstacles like escaping the orphanage at mid night and rushing in hurry towards railway station, she never saw the world so beautiful and quick outside and on her own toes with free soul, but even then she had a struggle buying tickets and catching the right train, which landed her up in wrong train but she made changes in the journey and somehow managed to be in Georgia( The place she always imagined) how would it look like, how would people see her as she already believed herself to be the highness of the dynasty.

Marcia carried great hopes as she carried herself to Roman cliff's charity show in North west, she wasn't going to the charity show but to get in the first conversation with Roman. Marcia already heard herself to be in the conversation with Roman cliff and she had a perfect plan to look like to most gorgeous girl to the duke, she wanted to convey the obsession of her life, a wish to see herself as Mrs. Roman cliff.

Her wish was not just a tramp imagination but a futuristic vision, a pulsating want, a keen wish and a beautiful reality which could have changed lives of many. The imagination she was creating in her mind since years and months was about to be true.

The doors opened wide and the man of her dreams entered in white overcoat and high boots, he was six feet 4 inches tall, with a cheerful face and humble demeanour, just the way marcia ever imagined. She stood at the last to have a meaningful and time conversation with

Roman and waited desperately for the charity show to finish. After good one-hour, roman cliff wrapped the show with his words and gestured to leave and within no time marcia ran into roman and asked him to be his partner, he misinterpreted something else and thought this girl is asking for a business opportunity and wants to be in partnership with him. Roman welcomed her gesture and decided to take her along after a conversation of good twenty minutes.

The valet opened the doors of Black Mercedes and Marcia and Roman entered the charity show hands in hands. After ten years marcia and roman were at the same place where they met for the first time and roman took marcia along after a misunderstood theory, this time the wish and imagination were a true reality and there they say every wish can be true if you had a heart in it, marcia was the duchess now, happily married to roman and a business partner with industrialist husband roman cliff group of companies. The true wish of Marcia had now become an absolute reality.

But how did all of this happen in just a spur of the moment?

Was it when roman and marcia met and marcia was all taken by roman along because of that misinterpreted thought and if that happened then how did the journey ended up here fulfilling Marcia's dream?

Or what was the story of these ten years from the present day?

Well, all these questions have a definite answer and Marcia made her wished true because she picked her goal thoughtfully, with a definite intention, she invested strong imaginative forces, all the worldly cosmic energies, her entire power and was focused on one imagination which she lived into reality, one true wish for which risked everything, she supported her goal with intense wish and all that was enough for her goal to become a beautiful reality that she was living every moment now with her endearing and only roman cliff.

To give you some background on those ten years......

After good ten months since marcia ran into roman and he misinterpreted the intentions thinking she is looking for a business partnership with him, marcia was desperately waiting for the right chance and was finally with that one-time fortune where she had to create her impression and let her true intentions make the appearance. To others, this would have been a routine chore of getting in Roman cliff's aisle, but in her mind, Marcia already imagined herself as a better half to roman every moment that she saw him standing in front and just wished truly for her and roman's togetherness, and this was her piece of mind and virtue of intentions from the very day she saw roman in the news article and Mr. Harvard taught her how to attract right people and things as he conveyed.

When Marcia finally had her golden chance with roman, she did not appeared needful and weak, nor did she tell him the story of her struggles and misfortunes of being an orphan rather she projected herself as a girl of faithful demeanour, she lived a better life staying in the industry of roman as an employee, she invested into her dressing style, her wardrobe, she always had a fascination of living life like a majority highness, and whatever frugal salary she had at that time, she could have imagined herself as a routine worker of degraded position and no good perks and money.

Usually, the employees of her position were weeping of inflation and not having enough as what they were getting from Roman group of companies, they only shared the thoughts of being born with insufficient resources and a compromising life, but marcia on the other hand was living in her imagination and was very happy to have some money and a great chance to meet and see her roman every moment, she used her money as an investment in herself and her personality so that she could make it to the Royal family. Maybe she was only inclined towards the glass half full and not half empty.

There is a strong belief in one thing that if you live well and invest in yourself, people notice and admire you and as you get this admiration every day, good things start coming to you.

Marcia made her true wish a reality because she wanted to be in Roman cliff more than she wished or imagined for anything else ever.

Marcia implanted a perfect goal in her mind and nurtured it with a purposeful imagination. And she never allowed her weaknesses and misfortunes to become obstacles and once she made her wish true, she never thought of her struggles and her past life as those were negative energies in her brand-new positive aura.

Ten years later, when one of her colleagues asked her, how did she do it?

What was this magic pill that brought her here as duchess to the charming duke roman?

She did not say, I "wanted "roman desperately and did everything I could to get him. Instead, she reverted, "Roman saw a business opportunity with me, we decided to get in partnership later and ultimately fell in love with each other.

There is a thing about imagined reality if you keep using certain words which belong to future then success and wisdom will always knock your door and will leave saying, might see you in future. So, if you really want it, make it your present imagined reality and not only a want of future, keep it closer and in present day to really make it your present.

Also, when Marcia was on determined journey to be with roman cliff and his empire, she never said to herself that, I will find something or someone else if I couldn't make it with roman. In fact, she always kept saying, I would move all the cosmic forces to get roman and a life with him and this is the only true wish of my life for which I will cross all the bridges and extend my limits.

"Marcia kept no options open for herself and the future, she had to win and only win"

And here is to Marcia and roman cliff's beautiful tale of love and companionship!

Having left with no options

It was in the middle of sixteenth century "Meh", a young boy in his late twenties loved a girl Susan very much. Finally, when they decided to share a lifetime with each other, Meh had to face Susan's father and convince him to marry his daughter, this scenario of convincing his father was been imagined by Meh several times but today it was the real day when he has to prove himself to fulfil his true wish of marrying Susan.

A long while ago, meh read somewhere that if you want to win someone or something then don't give them all the time to think and wonder, in fact just don't leave options for them as quick decisions are mostly in favour if you know the magic of influence. Meh planned a strategy to convince Susan's father in a way which made him necessary to come to a hasty decision. Meh got ready at 6'o clock with decent clothes in evening and left for church before Susan's father could arrive, he waited for him and as he arrived, meh sat next to him, he built some rounds of religious conversations and after prayers took him to father Joseph for blessings, father Joseph was already a part of the plan.

"It's the right time for you to get married my child" said father Joseph as he looked towards Susan, he further added - you will find your right man here today in the doors of our holy God who will fulfil all your wishes, listening to father Joseph's golden words Susan's father was curious to ask how will she get someone just here? Father joseph replied – The last man who comes to seek blessings of Christ after everyone else leaves from here would be Susan's man of honour, if she gets married to him, she will have a beautiful and blessed life else there is no marriage for her in this lifetime, so it's either today or never. Susan's father was a strong believer of prophecy and religion, he believed in father joseph's words as he had no other option listening to the ultimatum of father Joseph.

Susan's father and Susan stayed in the church after everyone else left, Susan knew everything about plan and was desperately waiting for Meh to arrive as the last person, she was imagining things and her life with Meh which was soon going to be a reality. After half an hour when everybody else left and there was all unsaid silence, A six feet tall boy with sheer innocence and sharp features arrived and bent down to offer prayers at the same spot where father Joseph told the guy would arrive, Susan's eyes started shining and she whispered to his father, Daddy – "here he is". Susan's father walked towards the young boy and asked him, hey you are the same wonderful man whom I was talking to in evening today, meh smiled and replied – yes sir, I left after the usual prayers but something brought me here as I felt some intense calling, I think God was remembering me.

Meh already influenced and impressed Susan's father by her religious conversations and now it was time for the magic of influence to yield results and convert imagination into reality. Susan walked to Meh and asked him, would you marry me? Meh was all surprised, at least he acted to continue the act.

Next week they got married in the same church and wished for their togetherness.

Magic of influence stays on if you believe in it.

Long ago, A billionaire in Yorkshire named Stephan got early success in career by launching a matchmaking website "happily together "and then investing the same money in many other businesses. Stephan was a young man surrounded by adorable women and would enjoy her life in every possible way, he had hook ups and breakup every now and then.

Stephan's mother "Rosie" was concerned seeing all of this as she always had one true wish that Stephan should learn to respect ladies and find true love. She tried to talk about this to Stephan but all in vain, but she didn't leave her hope and imagination of seeing her child happy with his wife.

One day Stephan received a call from his home that her mother is very ill and she wants to see Stephan here, listening to all of this Stephan left to meet his mother at the earliest as after all he truly had all the affection for her. On reaching home he sat near her mother and kissed her forehead, while doing so half-conscious mother hugged her son and asked him to do something for her.

With teary eyes and pounding heart Stephan asked, what can I do for you Mom? Tell me, I'll do whatever you may ask. Rosie was relieved listening to this and she asked him to get married to the girl of her choice and spent all his life with her, listening to such a wish, Stephan went into thinking but her mother asked Stephan to promise the same, he fell in short of words as it was almost impossible for Stephan to deny her bed ridden severely ill mother, who was just looking towards her son with hope that would not deny. After little thinking Stephan agreed and at the same moment Stephan and Liz vowed to stay together for life, Rosie was happy living her imagination turned into reality of seeing her son with his better half.

Initially it was hard for Stephan to accept Liz as his better half but gradually as they shared things and moments together, Stephan started building emotions for Liz and both fell in love. And today after five years in harmony, it's hard for Stephan to even imagine his life without Liz as they cut the cake for their fifth Anniversary and beautiful years of togetherness.

Do you think Stephan would have married to Liz, if his mother would have given him time and options?

Do you think Susan's father would have agreed to get his daughter married to Meh if father Jospeh would have left him with time and possible alternatives?

Every person who wins and makes decisions in any situation must be willing to erase his possible options and the calculated time for retreat. This is the only way to maintain the essential state of mind called intense wish & willingness towards win, the significant ingredients of fulfilling true wishes and transmuting imagination into reality.

If you can understand these ingredients well and know how to put them in the recipe of your imagined reality, all your wishes can be true.

As humans, we are all driven by wishes and hopes and only that we attain the understanding of this world so do we understand the necessity of being powerful and successful and that is where we start looking for ways to be wealthier more attractive more superlative in a sense of achieving fame and attention, we crave for a better and comfortable life, full of luxuries – having a big house, a sophisticated setting, a genre of beautiful relationships and an enriching society image. But just by imagining all these things and sitting back in harmony would not do any wonders but wishing what you want with a sense of never-ending confidence and a defined level of strategy in a way to execute and facilitate it will yield results in reality, also it's definitely been said that there is no way to a successful journey than having a sigh in patience and persistence, which will bring a success of permanence.

The recipe of success isn't that easy one as it looks like, it has a series of well-knit steps which are based on total ground reality of what we call practicality of life. As it says the very first ingredient to being successful and achieving goals is what do you exactly want? This could be money, material things, gems, jewellery, a car, a big house or a pair of branded shoes, could be anything.

Now when I say the word "exactly" it means that the thing has to be quantified like one, two or in terms of money a hundred million dollars or a lakh million dollars or anything else, if it's having a person define the exact qualities of the person you want to be with like – six feet tall or 5 feet 5 inches, white skin or yellow undertone, big eyes and soft muscular structure, whatever it is, it has to be well defined and the picture should be fixed in your mind just like Marcia had for Roman.

Second ingredient of this success recipe is to define the exact date when you want to have this particular thing to be accomplished or a goal to be fulfilled so if it is money then you should fix the date by which you will be a billionaire and will have ten billion dollars may be by 17th of July 2026 is the date. Nothing works without having a prescribed date and even the exact time for that matter, I remember my cousin Nancy was pregnant and wanted her baby to be born before 6 AM in morning as she considered this time holy and fortunate, she kept speaking to herself for all nine months that she wants to give birth in morning before 6 and the magic happened, her baby was born at exact 6'o clock in morning it was all unbelievable. So, dedicating a date and duration is very important ingredient this success recipe.

Next ingredient in the recipe is writing it clear and big in your own Diary, which is dedicated to only this particular goal, mentioning the concise statement of wish and the time duration by which you want to acquire it, The statement of words should be planned carefully as it should be similar each time that you write it and recite it, " it could be this way – I want to have a big house in the middle of northern

Pennsylvania which is fully furnished with Italian décor and fittings by March 2026 and I am living peacefully there with my family and kids.

Moving ahead, towards the last ingredient of the success recipe – you need now to plan, on how you can execute your goal on grounds and turn your imagination into sheer reality. Like if I want 100 million dollars by March 2026 then I would invest in more properties and will start making plans to arrange such meetings or I will gather money for buying a franchise or simply of have nothing I will start writing a book which will be sold for 40 million copies within a year, the point is there should be a perfect plan for ground work.

Please remember that if you could follow these wonderful steps as described above, you can definitely complete your recipe diligently and success will surround you from all the four corners, your goals seek a considerable discipline and dedication into practice.

Following these steps would not be an easy deal, at times you may complain that it is not at all possible to follow these steps and attract cosmic energies for the accomplishment of your goal, you may feel disappointed and out of optimistic zone or just refuse to believe in all of this but once you make it a habit of routine life, it will bring all the success to you sooner or later but for sure. "Never leave good habits and don't ever adopt bad habits"

While obeying these rules and habits of success recipe, people who are attracting money and luxury might complain that it is extremely hard to imagine wealth without actually having it, this is the exact turning point where you need to have strong imagination and true wish of converting you thoughts into reality and possessing real wisdom of whatever you truly wished for, we need to create an intense fire inside in order to believe what we wish for and you will see things turning in favour without even having second assumptions and thoughts.

As we discussed in first chapter of this book that "thoughts are things" here we need to understand that the if we can convince our mind for the success goal that we wish to achieve then gradually cosmic forces will align things in the direction where you will get to see a changed world and concepts around and within not time, everything that changed was truly conspiring for your success and wisdom, so learning to have a complete control over our thoughts is impossible but with a constant and calculated practice, this could be achieved and your success will be then decided by you and only you.

While talking to many successful people, living and working with them during different times in life, I've found and noticed a common factor that wealth comes to those who imagine it day in and day out and not just this it's a constant craving that they go through every day, they suffer failures and rewards both bigger and smaller but constantly practice their steps of success recipe without giving up on it because each time, we confront failure and are on the verge of disappointed and emptiness( which is possibly a common emotion of all humans) there is an another wide door of success or just a little hope emerging out of its shell and calling you to embrace it.

It's an usual practice of teaching subjects and focusing on grades in schools and universities, having varied disciplines and domains which are been researched and taught to students, this subject of becoming successful has no or very little presence anywhere and due to this conditioning of our society there is very less belief that people possess over such grounds of theories, it is highly believed that these theories are impractical and hypothetical with superlative impressions and no ground results. These steps of success recipe will be of great help to all those people who refuse to recognize the importance of imagination and true wishes.

These baby steps towards the success recipe are strongly been followed and applied by the author Shubhangi Saxena herself in routine life, towards better accomplishment of goals and wishes, after going through the various phases of following and applying these steps, she had understood the limits and boundaries of this success recipe, she knows where is it that things don't happen the way you want them and how there are hidden steps between the lines where you need to be careful.

But to share a fact, the steps discussed above are completely examined and approved by the author herself which cannot just create immense wealth but also bring the nicest and most rare opportunities of success to you, but in order to recognize that opportunity and transmute it in true wish, you need to read this book till last page.

Uncle Christopher's attitude towards wealth

There was a saying my uncle used to recite us every now and then that wealth can only be achieved by immense hard work and a lot of sacrifices, if you want to be rich, then put your blood and sweat, work day in and out for acquiring it.

Also, there is a major playing of your stars and fortune, if you are fortunate wealth will come but if you are not destined to have it then no amount of hard work and pain can bring wealth to you.

I was brought up by uncle Christopher, he was a man of daily wages, who would go to work come back at late night having some money and food in his hands as he arrived home, we would then cook meals and sleep, if I ever wished for anything of my choice then he would usually deny for that quoting" I work hard for meals of the day, and you have no idea how much hard work is put" how could have I even asked for anything of my choice. Seeing the attitude of my uncle, I always believed that wealth comes with a lot of undue struggle and hard work, it calls for great sacrifices on order to arrange for daily meals but beyond all these theories was an imagination which would strike my mind very often while I was sleeping or off to bed. The very imagination that inspired me to cultivate it into ground reality, I always wished for immense wealth and better life, but growing up with the mindset of uncle Christopher, I somewhere hesitated to reach out my imagination and true wishes.

On 13ᵗʰ July 2012, there was a huge conference where many celebrated Academicians and authors arrived, I somehow managed to get inside this big hall as I was really interested in writing.

After watching people receive appreciation and celebration, I too wished for a life they live and that's where I found myself delving into beautiful imagination of hopes and fantasies, Menon, A female voice from back called my name, I looked back and found a lady dressed in beautiful clothes and having straight blonde hairs walked up to me.
"Hi, I was looking at you while you were inside the hall grasping breaths of imagination" you heard right, those were the exact words that went deep inside and I was gazing at her in surprise like she knew the craft of reading minds.

Without wasting time, I told her my true wish of becoming wealthy and successful.

What she told me was to start believing in yourself and your instincts, imagine clearly in your head of what you exactly want, if it's wealth how much and within no time you will acquire it. She just gave a gist about some cosmic energies which keep circulating your imagination and wishes into universe and then it comes back to you in multiplied amounts.

After this once in a lifetime lesson, I returned home and couldn't sleep that night as it was a night of changed imagination and successful revelation. I started imagining things of having a lot of wealth in my head as a habit day and night as she told me, three weeks passed nothing great happened, I was living the same frugal life with my pessimistic uncle and trust me life was harsh.

After four weeks of considerable imagination, I suddenly recalled her words of what exactly do you want, and the game really started there.

While imagining wealth day in and out as a habit, I forgot to take note of her words, she told me to exactly imagine the amount or quantity of what I want, she also told me to write it down and start looking at it whenever you have time for thoughts in a day.

So simply without wasting any time, I imagined the exact amount of wealth I wanted to have and wrote it on a piece of paper, for next another four months nothing happened, neither anyone favoured me with extra money nor did I found anything which can make me wealthy. One fine morning when I was in bed and wondering what to do while reciting the wealth from that paper where I wrote it, I suddenly came up with an idea of having a bookstore as I was working for one already.

I did some research and started working on the idea believing that I am already in possession of a big book store, initially it wasn't easy but being a part of this kind of business, I never gave up and kept going. Today to which I own 100+ book stores in 20 cities and not just this, I have much more wealth than I ever imagined. And I think I have got this with a lot of consistent imagination and persistence as it finally is my reality. I truly wished for it and I have it and now it's your time!

The steps of attracting wealth and having material things as discussed earlier in the steps of success recipe demand no intense hard work or physical labour. It is written nowhere that success demands a considerable portion of sacrifices or asks one to behave unruly and crazy.

We read lot of disciplines in school and universities, it's good to be educated but for those who couldn't receive education due to poverty or lack of resources or any other reason, you need to know that becoming wealthy and all successful doesn't demand a degree or any formal education, it doesn't require you to be beautiful and attractive. I heard that no matter how good you are at your work but if you are unfortunate or not destined to acquire wealth and success goals, 'it is very unlikely that you get it as it is all about good fortune and great timings.'

But the reality describes, what is really needed to be wealthy and successful is a true wish for being wealthy, a great amount of imagination and belief in transmuting it to reality, having a true inclination and dedication towards achieving goal, living in hopes.

desires, veils and fantasies and just having enough planning and accumulating material resources for finally embarking your plans on. As all those who have acquired wealth in abundance just knew all the secret steps of cooking the recipe well and right.

For starters, it is imperative to note that one can never be wealthy and successful if he has not tried enough to gain grounds for the goal one wish to achieve, you desperately need to be working in and out by means of imagination and wish, palpitating wish and realistic imagination are two vital things apart from working towards the reality of turning it in favour. And more obvious thing is to believe in the path you have chosen for turning your imagination in reality and more.

In this subtle wisdom of turning your ultimate wishes into reality, you should never let pessimism or negative energies surround you and destroy the imagination of success thoughts as it is highly imperative for you to know that the finest of world leaders have accumulated great wealth are the people of thoughtful mindset and progressive approach who never restricted themselves from trying new opportunities or taking a pattern of risks, they always learnt things for their betterment and harnessed all the cosmic energies available for them with the wisest use of resources and optimism.

These people don't shy away in believing things and energies which are not visible and just practice turning thoughts and imagination into reality, the believe true wishes can be transmuted into real success if it's applied with the principles of success recipe, and these people are holding maximum wealth which is circulated in the entire system of financial world, they are the CEOs and Chairpersons of the most profitable pharmaceutical companies, real – estate ventures and conglomerates.

We are living in 21$^{st}$ century, and becoming rich here is just not a wish anymore its's an obsession, people can do anything in order to achieve wealth and success.

Keeping in mind this same thing we as the people of future success story need to know and keep abreast with the latest happenings and trends of success around the world as the process of being rich and successful is an imagined reality of many.

I heard Rachel trying her luck with the new literature book she just finished writing, she was thinking to sell it for good money to pay off all her debts and to make some extra money for enjoying the travel journeys this year. Bella on the other hand is featuring on Instagram as the most iconic fashionista of the month, she started Instagram blogging few months back and was really posting trendy looks in different clothing patterns, who knew that her posts would bring all the wealth and fame she was wondering while having the grasp. Mark on the other hand, Bella's brother know, was very much on Artificial intelligence and now he is getting funding worth millions from a US based company who want their work in their traces.

Here the world around is just getting all the new ways of making money these fewer examples mentioned above of Rachel, Bella and Mark are just nutshells people are going online for making money through selling cupcakes to home-made authentic pizzas, to giving salon services and everything else makes a contribution to the success stories we are been coming across nowadays, there are new a customizations, new wall moving picture art and new LED features, Anti dust ceiling fans, Germs killing wall paint to what not, we are in an era of making things till infinity and everywhere else. But beyond all of this, there is something which still makes sense and an inevitable ingredient of success recipe which is certain to be possessed and that is "what is the exact beginning and where is the end of it" even today we need to figure out the answer to this very question if we really want a difference and want to perceive things in our favour to the world, The awareness of where does one truly wishes to begin and what will be the last chapter once the goal is accomplished is a thing to be pondered upon and that is where you need to be cautious in making the right choice, but trust me it is not as difficult as finding a right husband for yourself or conceiving a baby in your womb, I think its way lesser troublesome than these kind of patience and perseverance seeking choices, the only right way to do it to begin there and don't stop until you accomplish it faithfully and successfully!

Remember the story of potluck?

The interesting story traces its roots from Middle Ages, primarily an impromptu meal served to unexpected guests or travellers. More of like drop in at the dinner hour to somebody's place would get you "the luck of the pot" which means whatever food was left over or kept on the simmer would be yours as you are the guest of the hour.

The world today is just like "Potluck" you may get served with opportunities everywhere and anywhere, at any hour and sometimes even you will realize it later. So here my friend is a tip you must remember, to win big in this wide world, you must never hesitate to step into the thing or opportunity you wish or like without having questions like why and how and what, because the more you will question the more confusion will arise and confusion clearly leads to misguidance and a lost path which we as goal-oriented opportunity seekers cannot afford, so this is where you need to catch up.

Hold the brush and paint canvas in your own way and put the paintings in exhibition, you never know you might get lucky to be the proud owner of highest selling painting. If you are all set to open a Chinese restaurant then don't wait just do the necessary planning and begin it over you might be the next Michelin star restaurant. The success recipe demands careful application of ingredients but all these ingredients need emotions and freedom of choice, you must know the spirit of the great success stories from the past, the dreams that is today's ultimate reality, the life that we are living today as reality was once a dream of those great pioneers who knew the ingredients of success recipe and applied it over with great human emotions and experiments of choice and they had freedom of hearts, because without it you can create great imagination and without great imagination there is no great reality.

We have airplanes today, we have great smartphones which have made our lives easier but do you know these weren't invented they emerged out of experiments and an urge of changing the world and making it a better place, we hear stories about every great discovery but there is an hidden emotion and a series of steps that a person go through every day while working on a goal, he applies the righteous principles but there is a constant hitting of that one emotion called my very own thing and trust me every human is simply building great things and pioneering around and into it.

We consistently need to market our talents and develop the real emotions for success. History speaks those who have got accolades are the people of real emotion and more talents than one can ever market, this spirit is the real shade of our human world our entire system.

Talking of past players and great pioneers for today, two great brothers Tom and James opened there first small outlet after considerable planning for which they could take over a small pizzeria called Domi Nick's Pizza. They believed in their unique business model of revolutionizing the pizza industry, they were trying a unique business model, the initial idea was not a simple journey, James and Tom had an struggle of eight months and much more as their business wasn't feeding enough for the losses and the outlet was brought on loan for which James was working as a postman, for this Tom and James could not split their work hours but Tom bought half of his brothers business by selling the pizza delivery vehicle. Nothing could have stopped Tom from achieving his big dreams and he went on to open two more stores, his funds might have got exhausted at times as losses are a part of any entrepreneurial journey but his true imagination and turning it to the reality of being the best pizza chain didn't get any sweat and pain, and today dominoes is one of the largest pizza chains in the world, you too are a dominoes fan, aren't you?

Do you know Stephan king?

A brilliant writer of more than fifty novels and 200 short stories was once been failure, his first book was dismissed like a garbage and was dumped, his wife pulled the plot out of the garbage and demanded to send it again. Today his writing is been considered as concrete rocks of a budding career, do you think he would have succeeded if has had given up during the struggle days.

Jeff Bezos had a series of struggling mistakes, he dreamt of creating a unique website but ended up having an array of failed ideas like an online auction site, an ultimately failed brand down the road became the repurpose idea of what we know as Amazon today!

Bezos could have easily dropped the idea of becoming the very disappointed person while going through these struggling patterns and suffering immense losses but he kept imagining his wish and today he is a proud owner of his very own reality Amazon.

The oracle was not just an easy stone of success, Lawrence Ellison dropped out of college and worked as programmer for good eight years while he was imagining his dreamy reality of having oracle after that he cofounded it with his boss but this was not it, after considerable struggles of years Ellison has to mortgage his house too in order to stay afloat in his business but due to constant constructive imagination and wishes of his truthful sense, he finally made oracle an achieving reality.

These stories are not just strong imagination turned realities but the epitome of excellence where the past dreamers knew nothing except how to do it and get everything to achieve their true wish.

You see this entire world is a better and opportunistic place for everyone, we have enough resources enough happiness abundant series of brighter imagination, the success stories are not just good for listening palate and praising these people, but it is about taking that first step and leaving the rest for the process, Bezos was sure about his imaginative idea or true wish but he was never sure of how to get it done by the process but although he was barely informed about the process he did not give up even after considerable mistakes and losses.

So what if Stephan king's first book was been treated as a pie of garbage but at least he tried his luck and followed his imagination of putting words into ultimate reality and no matter initially it was a doomed luck but later he became The Stephan king because of that failed writing, so everything that you come across while learning to walk on this journey, might be initial failures but these failures are the real stepping stones of a journey because the one who has never failed and has only succeeded is a person of God, yes humans are humans and we only succeed by failing and learning, making mistakes and celebrating small chores of success with dinners and treats.

Never be afraid of failures!

Always remember imagine big, make a wish for it until it becomes a reality and during this whole process never let laziness, hesitation or unnecessary pattern of thoughts surround you because you take any story from pioneers of past, all that they had in common was a true determination and staying away from negative emotions.

Feel positive to attract good things and success will hug you!

I met Kathrine last month, a lady who is running her successful beauty products store and now is enjoying her presence in 20 cities with the tag of just producing "Natural products". Her story is not that of a fancy movie who was born with silver spoon, or had a backing of her husband or relatives who funded her entire fad of having this beauty business, her initial days with this entrepreneurial journey was full of hardships. Her idea of having products with completely natural ingredients was rejected by everyone, but she stayed motivated because she herself suffered allergic reactions from one of the beauty products and had a had time getting better from it after spending dollars and meeting different dermatologists every now and then for one year.

She wouldn't have stayed this motivated if she herself hasn't been through those allergic reactions and suffering. "They say best things come to you only when you face worst of the circumstances" so was the case with Katherine, she knew she will have a tough time launching such products in market but her inner motivation kept her going and today she is where everyone dreams to be.

By the way, Kathrine gifted me the beauty products too when we catched up last month, they are pretty natural and amazing.

Nick would never have discovered his true passion of singing if he wouldn't have been bullied by his colleagues and batchmates all the time for singing the song at his boss's birthday eve. It was that angst and frustration of being bullied that he decided to do anything but not quit before being the most celebrated icon in the industry. And it's not that his journey was full of wishes and promises in fact nothing happened the way he imagined initially, he was rejected in auditions a number of times and again, he even left his job for pursuing the passion and had to lose all his savings in paying rent and surviving but after 3 years of constant push and pull he got his break and today people not just are his singing fan but applaud his personality of being the most affirmative celebrity singer.

We all have issues and problems around, we all have been bullied and insulted at times or once in a lifetime at least, but here we are, this is the moment of turning all the cosmic forces in your favour and let them create the magic of imagined reality to you. So never talk of quitting work or switching work organization or moving cities for that matter as you think people are bad and weird here instead find out that real wish of yours and just make it happen with whatever resources you have in hand, I know this will sound very impractical and unrealistic but if you are been bullied or mistreated by someone promise, don't lose heart or be disappointed instead imagine you being the boss of the bigger company you are working with or just think of the life you want in order to be the person of all the wealth and comforts so that nobody can mistreat you, I know it sounds like being on an ego trio but trust me these innate forces can bring the most awaited and imagined breakthroughs in life if you know how to channelise your own emotions in the righteous direction.

Uncle Joseph always wished to make great money and fame, he use to meditate and imagine himself in the shoes of great entrepreneurs but did nothing but distributing newspapers and magazines to make living, something inspired him to the depths of heart while observing the process for good ten years and today he owns a chain of magazine stores at south Westland.

Liza always imagined herself as an iconic singer but wasn't confident enough about her singing skills until she was forced by destiny to sing in the streets of Barcelona in order to arrange meals for the family and one fine day when she met with Popins "The Singing sensation of the country" it was a moment of changed lifetime, today she sings for even movies.

At times we are constantly forced to do things out of poverty or for survival but you never know when destiny has a plan for you and it could change your true wishes and ultimate imagination into a beautifully turned reality. But the principles just ask for something called dedication and persistence into practice.

They say there is a difference between just making a wish and transforming it into reality, to explain further, if you are just making a wish with closed eyes and meditative mind to acquire the clothing store near your house, it's just wish but when you start making efforts by entering that clothing store, getting into conversations with people, buying their fabrics and garments, finding their weaknesses and competitors and finally learning the craft of running business, imagining your presence there as an owner and main person that is when you are actually making efforts along with the wish to convert it into reality of given purpose.

Always remember to be intact on your crucial self and keep your shrimping self-float with dreams and vibes as no great effort is demanded for setting higher goals in life or for achieving success and prosperity than to be in the situation of hugging misfortune and frugality.

True wishes have a perfectly laid imagination

True wishes can even force nature to change the destiny, I always loved spending summers at my cousin's place and this summer I planned to revive the old memories of childhood by finally landing up at the cousin's place. Reaching up there I realised that things weren't same like early childhood days as two of my cousin brothers shifted from here and only one cousin was living here with his five -year daughter Myra, Myra was born with a condition of leg deformity wherein she was declared unable to walk on her feet by expert doctors and might remain this way for life so she came into this world with legs but there was no sensation to be able to walk. My cousin and his father had a pressed opinion of the most advanced surgeons even but the declaration was same, that the child would not be able to walk for life.

After having known this magic called "The imagined reality" for all the years I did not believe what doctors had to say about Myra, but the disadvantage was I could not have had expressed this opinion and wish to Myra's father as I was only a cousin of him, but that doesn't mean I would have stayed quiet and wouldn't have had turned a stone for my niece's well-being, I expressed my opinion but in silence, in my own mind I imagined Myra walking towards me with her two little feet and hugging me, I told myself that Myra would be fine very soon and will live life like an enriched soul with all the normal activities.

In my heart and my strong determined mind with full of positive imagination, I knew that my cute Myra would be able to walk and even run very well. At that time the thought of those great words of my mum where she said" everything is possible if you ask for something with true wish and selfless heart" we just have to trust the process and give our best and I knew I would be able to find a way, just that right way!

During that time, I was working as a freelancer with some newbies corporation and mostly the work was done over laptop, so I decided to stay back here with my cousin and little Myra and get her out of this troublesome life, while going through the varied principles of this chapter we learned that the first thing is to know " what do you exactly want" , So here in more than anything else during that phase of my life I imagined that my little Myra should not stay with the current condition of leg deformity and she should run towards me holding her beautiful white doll that she used to hold all the time, and from that picture in my mind and exact thought in my heart I never budged, not even for a moment, I kept that exact thought and the picture alive.

Every minute there was just one thing on my mind that what could I do about making Myra's condition be better? Anyhow I had to transplant this intense imagination into Myra's mind that she should walk like others and she should have strong burning desire of conveying this positive vibe into the motions of her little naughty mind.

Myra was like other kids except for the fact that she could not run and walk like others and was needed with help to change and take bath and do her routine activities. And just like other kids she wanted to run and lead a normal life but maybe she never implanted an intense imagination in her mind of being able to walk.

In the first few days, I tried to be friends with Myra as only when she would be able to cooperate with me to fill her mind with the most intense imagination and a wish to run, jump, walk and be just like the most wonderful kids of her age, I knew that by doing so the cosmos would transmute her imaginative goals into true ground reality of her life. All of this rice dish with different lentils and spices was cooking on in my mind since the very day but I didn't spoke of it to anybody. Every morning I used to wake up having the goal just in front of my eyes that today Myra would be taking her first step in faith and would be able to do some activity on her own.

After three months as she turned a little older, she started taking my imagination into her perspective of little mind and that was the day of a gradual but hopeful beginning.

One fine evening, I began playing a game in front of her where the use of legs was important, she observed it initially and started getting into some thinking, and that's where I could see the success of implanting the seed, the desire to be able to walk and use legs, on that day though she made no attempt for trying to walk or stand up but I could see her thinking pattern and observations were going in the direction positively. And that's where I could see the result of my long efforts. Here the important thing to note is having patience and never stopping your efforts until success is achieved.

Usually when we are determined to start making a change or striving for better things, we often find ourselves demotivated and disappointed either by time taking process or initial failures, and that is just the beginning of something called success journey, so keep going my friend!

Next week after a little change in her mind, I began playing a movie which talked about a girl with similar issues and how she conquered it and now was a part of baseball team. Myra watched it little reluctantly but soon she kind of started to enjoy more and more. She was gradually diving into ecstasies and wonders of being all capable to walk and run, I could see that gradual imagination turning reality. One fine night she started playing that movie herself and watched it with all the heart like she is the winning character of her own movie.

This led to the arousal of this lazy will of hers which asked her to try being on her feet. In mere silence I saw her trying to stand with the support of her wheelchair. Watching this determination and wish to be able to walk and lead a normal life like other kids, I started planting my imaginative thoughts into her mind. I observed that she likes to dress up, this one good and positive factor can be turned into a motivation, I started getting her beautiful barbie dresses and began dressing her like a doll, every evening soon after finishing my daily routine work, I would create a theme and dress Myra like a doll and then would ask her to show how she looks standing straight. Though results weren't there on a clear verge but I could figure out that she is trying her level best.

Days after days I kept doing the same thing constantly implanting in her mind and telling her that she can walk and run anytime she truly wishes for it, I was always encouraging her to never believe that she is incapable in some sense in fact I used to tell her how she is planning to be a great dancer and an athlete of her own kind as she is saving her energy to kickstart the career on a much better note as others have wasted it all the while and she has conserved for the years, so the moment she would come on field she would appear with all the flying colours and would nail it truly and really.

At the same time, I was also reminding her that it's already been years that she has conserved the energy for the bigger and better game and now she should focus on appearing in the row.

As I went ahead on this journey of implanting right direction imagination and favourable thoughts in Myra's mind, I could see that immense believe that she gained in herself and in me over the time and this is the right opportunity so make things better for me and to make her believe that she is a person with opportunities and advantages also letting her feel belonged and loved.

To begin with I decided to take her for dance classes every day, on finding this decision I thought she would revolt and freak out, but she did not question my decision at all, maybe she had a firm believe in me and has accepted my identity in my life as a healing coach. Taking advantage of the very same belief that she had in me, I taught her the opportunities and merits she is born with and how she can utilize it to the best in her favour, Myra was always fond of listening praises about herself to an extent that she would start taking positive baby steps if compliments are on her way. Keeping the same thing in mind, I thought of utilizing it so I told her that she is different and better than other kids of her age because she is unable to walk and people would lend her special attention as she is unable to dance and walk, during her first day of dance class Myra had the same thing in mind and she received special concern and care of the dance academy teachers and few students, Myra was happy to have been recognized and have received the identity of someone being known and accepted by the people other than I and her Father. I started teaching her how she can turn tables in favour by being the person of her own identity, she kept going to the dance classes for a week and tried steps sitting and wondering if she could do it on her feet too. Yes I know that she was wondering deep down inside, so to give you a background, why would I implant this thing in Myra's mind that she should be comfortable and keep receiving sympathy when I myself took oath to make her feet fine soon, well as I mentioned earlier Myra loved compliments, she kind of always found motivation for doing things in a better way by having people's back and a sense of feeling belonged, not just this Myra would also like to extend her limits to keep that praises and compliments for longer by being people's favourite. So that is where I played cards with her. Slowly and gradually on every dance lesson I started implanting this imagination of being the best dancer in the academy and being applauded with compliments and wishes, I taught her how to start sowing the seed for the power of imagination, that she is dancing on the same stage where everyone else was demonstrating the skills of dancing. She started imagining her face and herself in the kids performing there sitting away and watching the performances and rehearsals one after the other. They seem to have been preparing for the final competition in a dance festival which was 3 months from now. Myra and I were discussing the same that how could she receive applaud and awards from more people and I suddenly barged into her little inquisitive mind why don't you also participate and dance the best on your feet in this dance festival.

Myra was six years old by this time and could understand and interpret well what is said, previous Myra would have surprisingly asked me?? What are you saying but this new Myra since I taught her things, was a different version of herself. She didn't question my words instead said, well I think I can try, I felt astounding with happiness listening these golden words from My little Myra. I told myself the fruits are about to appear in the plant I sowed a year later when she was five.

I was sure that she would be able to walk on her feet within these three months, as her legs as per the doctors were fine but she didn't had sensation to be able to feel beneath her bottom, I just was working towards awaking her willpower which could bring sensation into her organs at the very bottom of her body.

Myra fell several times from the chair while trying to be able to walk, she got minor injuries too but I don't know how but she was just determined to dance in that festival and would probably do everything she could to get that award. She didn't lose hope and kept trying every day, seventy days passed and I couldn't see any improvement in her condition and after this point even I felt like giving up seeing little Myra this way, but as "they say the moment you think this cannot happen it definitely happens" because you've put all of your worthy energies in the retrospect.

On the day of this dance festival Myra juggled with things and got ready in attire, Myra was called up on stage and she appeared in the same way sitting and performing, I lost my hopes as my implanted imagination could not become her beautiful reality, I cursed myself for all the things I did and promised to accept her the way she is. But in that moment of agony and sadness something unexpected happened and Myra's name was called up for the award of being the most versatile and confident performer, before I could help her with the thing, she was balancing her soles standing up on feet and trying to take step ahead, I helped her with the balance and with immense agony but a smile of satisfaction and being normal like others she marched towards the stage and received the award. Every person looked at her with surprise even I could not believe what I just encountered. But it wasn't my imagination but a heart filled true reality.

Agony and laziness is the spouse of every individual, be it child or an adult, but by applying the few principles of Assertiveness and mental agility one can conquer all the weaknesses with flying colours and let the aura shine in optimism and immense faith of being.

We humans live in a world made up of planets, stars & galaxies, A world which is full of abundance and if you trust then there is no scarce. We have enough for each one of us and these magical resources for which call 'True wishes or Imagined reality' never reduces of lessens, it just keeps adding in abundance as we practice the principles of cosmic energies.

In this era of abundance and realizing the power of cosmos, we also need to know that cosmos around us identifies only optimism, victory and success, it does not recognize pessimism, uncertainty, frugality and failures. So, this is the time for us and we should leave no stone unturned in the practice of successful being in everything and anything.

Just like Myra learned how to utilize her energies in imagining prosperity & abundance of what she could accomplish by standing on her own feet instead of brooding on what her life is without being able to walk. I always implanted the thoughts of completeness and positivity in her mind instead telling her the weaknesses and letting her count on them for life. Myra could walk because she always knew she can, I never let he know what doctors have to say about her condition or what people and other kids would have whispered on her back about her inabilities instead I told her to see what is right and true for her betterment and rest you know the verdict.

In our course of this beautiful and hectic life, we often forget the word Miracle, yes miracles still exist and they keep happening to you while you understand and live this very word. But the principles of success recipe also tell that these miracles only work when you believe in it and truly ask for something from the cosmic power. Implanting thoughts and imagining them consistently can force the energies to turn in your fruitful favour, all we need is to imagine with persistence, wish with faith and wait in patience, miracles will come your way to turn everything into a wise possession, everything will be a true reality.

So just keep believing in yourself!!

True wishes come true only when you make a wish with all that honest and faithful heart filled with the deep imagination of success and being celebrated.

#3

<u>OVERCOMING FEAR OF FAILURE</u>

(It stays with everyone so learn to deal with it)

So, as we begin with this third chapter of our constantly reviving journey to the imagination and reality, let's learn about some biggest enemies of our success journey, they call them "Fears". Any wonder why am I calling it them?? Well for starters, I believe fear is not a single entity to be mustered upon in fact it's a close-knit series of many unnecessary forces which keep haunting us, keep creating doubts and blemishes in our mind about any decision that we take. Learning to overcome them is something that we need to learn or teach our minds; it begins by a clear and concise understanding and then learning or figuring out different solutions to be imposed in order to move ahead of "them"

You know there are call by names too for these unnecessary forces like confusion, depression, darkness, unruly things and people, dissatisfaction, future happenings, current failures, poverty, ill health, separation, denial, anger, insult, sadness, death, misfortune, torture, physical abuse and much more. We all must have faced or must be facing this call by names at a point in life, but do you know these unnecessary forces can be defeated with the emergence and patience of hope and appropriate action. For imposing a solution and creating a better and beautiful reality out of our beloved imagination, let's understand these fears first.

Let's begin with our first fear "confusion" often called as having a pool of unnecessary options or the fear of having haunting results on picking either

# Contents